Bird Buddies

A Curious Tale of Feathered Friends

written and illustrated by

Kenton R. Hill

{with help from Rosa Rodriguez}

LUMINARE PRESS

WWW.LUMINAREPRESS.COM

Bird Buddies
A Curious Tale of Feathered Friends
Written and illustrated by Kenton R. Hill © 2017

Printed in the United States of America

Cover and Interior Design by Claire Flint Last
Author Photo by Ed Keene

Luminare Press
438 Charnelton St., Suite 101
Eugene, OR 97401

www.luminarepress.com

ISBN: 978-1-944733-39-1

"Differences are not intended to separate, to alienate. We are different precisely in order to realize our need of one another."

—DESMOND TUTU

To my brothers, Kelly, Doug and Gary, who have been my life-long buddies and fellow birdwatchers.

Contents

Bird Buddies

-1-

The Hideout

"It zips away every time. I can hear it, but I can never get close enough to see it.

"That's why I built this hideout. I've got my dad's binoculars, and I'm ready to climb in," Rosa said to her friend, Boone. "Wanna join me?

"You'll have to stay very still and be very quiet. I know that won't be easy for you, but you will have to if we are ever going to see it."

Boone agreed and joined Rosa in her hideout. They really wanted to catch sight of that speedy little hummingbird Rosa had been hearing in her backyard.

Rosa was right to be worried about inviting Boone to join her in the bird-watching hideout.

"There it is!" Boone shouted as soon as the hummingbird flew in their direction.

"There it was!" Rosa sighed. Boone's shout had scared it away. It was several minutes before the hummingbird returned. As it did Boone shifted inside the box to get a better view. He bumped into Rosa and caused the hideout to shake, once again sending the hummingbird quickly away.

When the hummingbird arrived for a third time Boone managed to sit still and stay quiet long enough to watch it hover in mid-air, feeding on a bright red flower.

Boone couldn't help himself. He whispered to Rosa, "That's so cool." But, watching the hummingbird eat reminded Boone he hadn't had lunch. When the hummingbird whizzed away again, he slipped out of the hideout to go home and make a sandwich.

"I'll bring you something when I come back," he announced to Rosa, who was happy to stay, watching, and making notes about what she was seeing.

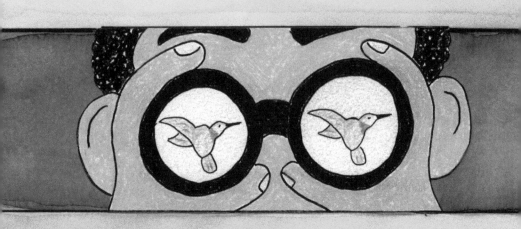

By the time Boone returned with a sandwich for Rosa, she had quite a long list of things she had noticed while watching the hummingbird's actions. They continued to be still and watch quietly, easier for Boone now that his stomach was not growling. He too was becoming curious about this little bird that was like a bullet with wings.

As the list grew longer, Rosa finally said, "Let's go see my aunt and tell her what we've seen so far. She's an ornithologist."

"An ornery what?" Boone asked.

"Not ornery—an ornithologist. That's a scientist who studies birds. She'll be impressed with our bird watching. 'Birding' as she calls it. Let's go see her."

The Good Question

"Hi, Aunt Olivia," Rosa called out as they arrived at her aunt's science lab. " My friend, Boone and I have been spying on a hummingbird, and we have a list of all the things it can do. Wanna see it?"

"I sure do. Show me."

BIRD WATCHING NOTES

1. Hovering like a helicopter
2. Poking skinny beak into flowers
3. Scares other birds away
4. Catching tiny bugs in mid-air
5. Flies fast — up, down, zigs, zags, backwards, forwards, upside down
6. Never walks or hops — only flies and sits still
7. More time perching than flying

Aunt Olivia was impressed with all they had seen just by being quiet and watching carefully. "Very good job for a couple of young scientists."

That last note on the list reminded Rosa of another thing she saw. "He landed on the wire and just sat there scratching his head for a long, long time."

"Birds do spend more time preening than flying. They need to keep their feathers looking nice and ready for flight," Aunt Olivia added.

"We also saw him fly up to a string of Christmas lights. Our neighbors still have them hanging from their roof. He flew right up to the red bulb like it was a flower," Boone recalled.

"That can happen. Hummingbirds aren't attracted to flowers so much by their scent, but more by what they look like. And red is their favorite color," Aunt Olivia explained.

All of this talk was making Rosa and Boone anxious to get back to their work as junior scientists to see what more they could learn about this fascinating little bird.

But, as they headed for the door they were surprised to see Aunt Olivia had a new birdcage in her lab.

When Aunt Olivia noticed Rosa's and Boone's interest in her new bird, she said, "That's an African Grey Parrot."

They paused to take a good look. It was a much different bird than the humming-bird they had been watching.

African Grey Parrot

She told them she had rescued it from a pet store so she could care for it and learn all she could about this very intelligent and talkative bird. She offered Rosa a book to read so she too could learn more about parrots and hummingbirds.

They thanked Aunt Olivia, and as they were leaving, Boone and Rosa talked about the differences in these two birds. Almost everything they could think of was different. Boone wondered out loud, "Do you think they could ever be friends like you and me, Rosa?"

"Good question." The parrot said.

"That is a good question," Rosa repeated.

It was a good enough question to inspire Rosa to go home and begin to write a story. *The Story of Hector and Penda.*

The Story

Rosa had fun over the next several days writing and drawing. When she was finished she stopped by Boone's house and asked him to come with her to see Aunt Olivia again. Rosa was anxious to share her story with her best friend and her ornithologist aunt.

Rosa began to read…

THE STORY OF HECTOR AND PENDA

Written and Illustrated by Rosa Rodriguez

Hector was humming along flying past an open window when he heard, "Hummmm hummmm," coming from inside.

It surprised Hector. He paused in mid-air (hummingbirds can do that you know) and he hummed, "Huh?"

Then he heard the voice again coming from a parrot (parrots can do that you know), "Want a cracker?" she asked.

Hector, the hummingbird, was not interested in a cracker so he replied, shaking his head, "Uh uh."

Penda, the parrot, tried again, "Want a red flower?"

To that, Hector screeched to a halt, flew in the window, perched on Penda's cage, nodded his head in favor and hummed, "Uh huh!"

That is how this strange and unlikely friendship between Hector the hummingbird and Penda the parrot began.

How did Penda know Hector would like a red flower, you ask?

The answer is that Penda lives in a cage in a science lab with a woman who is an ornithologist. Ornithologists know lots of interesting things about all kinds of birds. So, Penda just sits and listens carefully, which she does all day since there's not much else to do when you live in a cage.

When the scientist says, "That's interesting," Penda perks up, listens, and learns. That's how she knew Hector would like a red flower.

Hector remained perched on Penda's cage. Waiting for the promised red flower, but there were no flowers in sight. Finally Penda said, "Outside," and pointed her wing toward the window.

"Huh?" Hector wondered.

"Flower. Outside." Repeated Penda. "Let's go!"

Like most hummingbirds, Hector is a very shy and independent bird. To him Penda looked so large and so strong, and she could even talk. Hector is really, really small and can only chirp, click, and hum. He didn't know what to do.

Penda and Hector just sat there staring at each other. They stared for a very long time. Until Hector, who was getting hungry and really wanted the nectar in that red flower, stopped being afraid of this big bird with the bright red tail and scary beak and decided to open the cage and let Penda out.

Hector used his long skinny beak to pick the latch on the cage freeing Penda to fly out the window. Hector quickly followed.

Hector was surprised that even as small as he was he could fly as fast as a parrot.

As they flew together, Hector was just humming along while Penda was talking and talking — telling Hector all of the interesting things she knew about hummingbirds. Facts she had learned listening to her scientist caretaker.

- COME FROM SOUTH AMERICA
- THAT'S INTERESTING
- WEIGH ABOUT THE SAME AS A NICKEL
- FLY 500 MILES WITHOUT STOPPING
- THAT'S INTERESTING
- WINGS FLAP 200 TIMES PER SECOND
- LARGE HEART
- THAT'S INTERESTING
- BIG BRAIN

Hector is so busy all day sipping nectar, eating bugs, pollinating flowers, grooming his feathers, chasing off his enemies all by himself that he doesn't know half of what Penda knows about what a unique little bird he is.

It made Hector feel good to think Penda knew so much about him. He even began to wonder what was special about her.

It was a good thing the garden Penda had seen from her window wasn't too far away. She had been in the cage so long she was out of practice. Penda couldn't fly as far or fast now as other parrots in her family back in Africa.

When they arrived at the garden, Hector watched Penda crunch on greens while he hovered among the most delicious red flowers he had ever seen.

After lunch Penda had another
interesting fact to tell Hector,

   —   YOU CAN FLY UP 100 FEET...

   —   ...THEN DIVE AT 60 MILES PER HOUR.

Hector knew that fact and proudly
hummed, "Uh huh!" Then took off.

Climbing to a height of 101 feet. Then, like a rollercoaster, he turned and dove toward the ground at 60 miles per hour. Just as Penda had said. It is a trick Hector uses to get the attention of female hummingbirds.

Just before he came to the ground, Hector quickly pulled up, hovered, and hummed over Penda, who was for once, speechless.

-4-

The Trick

Rosa paused in the reading of her story to see if Aunt Olivia and Boone were still interested, and they were.

"Is all that true what Penda is telling Hector?" Boone asked Aunt Olivia.

"Oh yes, hummingbirds are special little birds. Like Penda said their hearts and brains are among the largest of any bird—considering the size of their bodies. And they do weigh a little less than a nickel."

Boone had another question, "Can they really fly 500 miles without stopping?"

Rosa, who had read the book Aunt Olivia had given her in preparing to write her story, answered Boone's question, " Yes, many Ruby Throated Hummingbirds do that twice a year. They fly back and forth over the Gulf of Mexico between the United States and Mexico and on to Central America."

"Rosa, how does your story end? With all of their differences – coming from different countries, their sizes, shapes, colors, their different languages – do Penda and Hector become friends like you and me?" Boone was anxious for an answer to that "good question" Aunt Olivia's parrot asked earlier.

"If you are quiet and sit still like you had to do in the hideout, I will finish my story," Rosa said with a smile.

Hector's amazing dive was shocking to Penda. She had heard about how hummingbirds could do that but had never seen it done. As she watched, she was a bit jealous.

"I want to try it." Penda announced.

Hector was surprised to hear Penda say that. He wasn't sure it was even possible for a parrot to do such a thing. So, he shook his head and hummed, "Uh uh!"

But Penda ignored Hector's warning. She flapped her wings. Took a deep breath and began the climb. Because she was out of practice, she couldn't quite make it up to 100 feet. But, when she got as high as she could fly, she turned and started her dive.

Faster and faster she fell toward the ground. And just at the last minute she began to pull up. But, she must have waited one last minute too many, because instead of successfully lifting back up into the air, Penda plopped flat on the ground.

Hector quickly flew over to where Penda had landed. He was sad to see she wasn't moving and one of her wings looked broken. Hector knew he was too small to carry Penda. He wondered how he could ever get her back home to her cage.

Well, yes hummingbirds are small, but remember they have big hearts, so they aren't going to leave an injured friend behind. And also remember they have big brains so they are smart enough to figure out how to do it.

Hector knew he would have to fly back to the lab where Penda lives and let the scientist know Penda needed her help.

But, before he left Penda lying there on the ground he looked around for any sign of danger. Any other animals that might want to harm a helpless parrot. He spotted a chubby old cat trying to hide behind a tree.

Then using his famous diving trick that was not only good for attracting females, but also good for scaring away enemies, he flew up and up, dove quickly down, beak open, claws out, and sent the cat scurrying away.

Knowing he could not talk like a parrot, could not tell the scientist about what had happened to Penda, Hector pulled one red feather from Penda's tail before he hummed back to the lab as fast as he could fly.

As Hector dropped the feather at the scientist's feet, she realized he knew where her missing parrot had gone and knew she needed to follow Hector's lead back to Penda. She hopped into her car and did her best to keep up with Hector as he flew back to rescue Penda.

Safely back in her cage, Penda was thankful Hector's big heart and big brain worked so well together.

As she looked over at Hector, who was perched on her cage, she was thinking about how sometimes a small act of kindness can spark a friendship. And she thought that maybe she and Hector would discover they are more alike than different.

Penda smiled at Hector and said, "Thank you."

Hector smiled back, hummed, and dropped one of his red feathers into Penda's cage. Then he picked up the feather from Penda he had used to tell the scientist he needed her help, and flew back to those delicious red flowers Penda had found for him.

"The end," Rosa finished reading her story.

Boone couldn't wait to say, "I love your story. It's exciting and fun to hear!"

"I agree," Aunt Olivia added. "You have paid close attention, and have learned lots of interesting things. Nice work, Junior Scientist. Way to go, Story Teller.

"But, you do know hummingbirds don't really hum through their beaks. It's their wings that make the humming sound."

"That's interesting!" her parrot commented.

"And," Aunt Olivia went on, "you know, a hummingbird couldn't really understand what a parrot was saying. Birds and animals can't really..."

Rosa interrupted her aunt, "Are you sure? Haven't you read The Owl and the Pussycat? Peter Rabbit? Winnie the Pooh?"

To that the parrot added, "Ornithologists can't know everything."

Aunt Olivia smiled and said, "Okay. Okay, you may just be right. So, what's next?"

"Back to the hideout." Rosa answered.

Boone agreed, "Back to the hideout!"

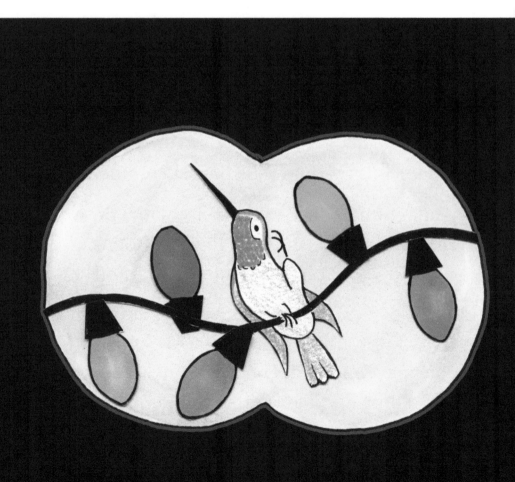

5

The Facts

Here are some more facts about hummingbirds that I learned while watching and reading about my feathered friend, Hector...

1. Hummingbirds originally came from South America. They now live from Chile to Alaska.

2. Hector is a South American name that means tenacious (determined, tireless, and strong-minded).

3. There are more than 340 different kinds of hummingbirds (14 different kinds regularly live in North America, but another 13 have shown up at least once).

4. Females build the nest (half the size of a golf ball), lay and protect two white eggs (half the size of a jelly bean). These eggs look like brown raisins and hatch in about 16 days. Then the little birds fly off on their own in less than a month.

5. Male hummingbirds don't help the females build the nests or take care of the baby birds.

6. As babies their enemies are mostly other birds like blue jays and crows.

7. As adults they are pretty good at out-flying other birds, but have to be careful to avoid spider webs, bees, wasps, snakes, praying mantises, squirrels, and chubby old cats.

8. Hummingbirds are very independent. They mostly live alone.

9. Hummingbirds come in different sizes. Ruby Throated Hummingbirds (like

Hector) weigh about the same as a nickel. Giant Hummingbirds weigh more and Bee Hummingbirds (the smallest birds in the world) weigh less.

10. Ruby Throated Hummingbirds are about 3 inches long with a wingspan of 3 to 4 inches.

11. Their wings can beat as fast as 200 times per second. Their wings can move in a figure eight pattern so they can hover and fly backwards. They are the only bird that can do that.

12. Every 10 to 15 minutes they eat nectar, tree sap, pollen, or insects (eating two times their weight every day).

13. If I (an 8 year old girl) ate as much as a humming bird, I would have to eat 110 pounds of food a day.

14. While they sip the nectar (through their very, very long forked tongues) they are also pollinating between 1,000 and 2,000 flowers a day.

15. Their feet have 4 toes (3 in front and 1 in the back).

16. Ruby Throated Hummingbirds fly south in the fall and back north in the spring (up to 500 miles at a time without stopping, with the help of the wind). They have to leave the cold, snowy places every winter because their food is gone.

17. Their average flying speed is 30 miles an hour — up to 60 miles an hour when doing their diving trick.

18. Their normal body temperature is 105 to 108 degrees Fahrenheit except when sleeping. Then it goes down to 70 degrees Fahrenheit.

19. Their heart beats 250 times a minute while resting — about 1,260 times per minute when flying.

20. They like to sleep on small twigs at the end of branches, where it is harder for their enemies to reach them.

21. Hummingbirds have about 940 feathers (fewer than other birds, but more per square inch than all other birds). Their feathers are replaced every year.

22. Their feathers are only black, brown, and reddish brown. The bright red and green colors are just a reflection of light.

23. They have an extra eyelid (like goggles) to protect their eyes when diving at 60 miles per hour.

24. They like to take baths more than most birds. Mostly they like shallow moving water or spray mist baths.

25. Hummingbirds live from 1 to 9 years. The record is 12 years.

And I also learned a lot about my other feathered friend, Penda, the African Grey Parrot.

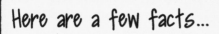

Here are a few facts...

1. Many parrots come from South America, but the African Grey Parrot comes from the forests of Central Africa.

2. Penda is an African name that means beloved.

3. There are more than 350 different kinds of parrots.

4. Females build nests in tree cavities and lay three to five eggs which take about 30 days to hatch.

5. In the wild, monkeys and snakes like to eat parrot eggs.

6. Both parents take care of the chicks until they leave the nest in 12 weeks. Then the young parrots hang around for a year or so.

7. Parrots live in groups — as many as 20 or 30 in a group. But, at night you might see as many as 100 sleeping high in a tree.

8. Staying in groups helps keep them safe from enemies like eagles and hawks and very large snakes. They defend themselves by fluffing up their feathers to look bigger, flying fast, and biting if they have to.

9. Parrots mostly live in one area throughout their adult life.

10. African Grey Parrots are some of the largest parrots in Africa.

11. An adult weighs about one pound.

12. They are about 13 inches long with a wingspan of 18 to 21 inches.

13. Parrots are different from other birds because they have strong curved beaks, and their feet have four toes (2 in front and 2 in back).

14. Like hummingbirds, parrots also have large brains compared to their body size.

15. Parrots can fly between 30 and 40 miles per hour, but are not good at diving.

16. They are in danger of becoming extinct in Africa because people capture them to sell as pets or to sell their feathers.

17. In the wild, they eat flowers, fruit, seeds, leaves, roots and soil. As pets they eat fruits, vegetables, nuts, seeds, and bird pellets.

18. A pet parrot can be fun, but you need to be very sure you can and will be able to take good care of it.

19. Just like people, parrots have different personalities (from shy to outgoing – from serious to comical).

20. They need a lot of exercise (2 to 3 hours a day) outside their cage to stay strong and healthy.

21. Parrots also get bored easily so they need lots of different toys to play with.

22. They can mimic people, but also mimic birds, animals and other sounds.

23. African Grey Parrots are very intelligent – as smart as 4 to 6 year-old children in some ways like knowing words, objects, colors, and shapes.

24. A famous parrot, named Alex, learned over 100 words.

25. Parrots can live from 50 to 80 years as pets, but live only about 23 years in the wild.

6

Hummingbirds at Home

As Rosa and Boone learned, many hummingbirds migrate between where they spend the winter and the place where they raise their young. Scientists are studying them to find out more about the migration paths they follow and to learn which flowers they drink from as they fuel up on nectar.

While hummingbirds sometimes eat small insects and spiders, their favorite food by far is the sweet liquid called nectar that is produced inside some flowers. A hummingbird may visit 2,000 flowers in one day in search of nectar.

Many people attract hummingbirds by planting flowers hummingbirds like. Others hang up hummingbird feeders.

Some people are helping with scientific research through a project called "Hummingbirds at Home." These citizen scientists keep track of the hummingbirds they see, as well as which flowers provide them with nectar, and report their findings through Audubon's free app or website.

Observing hummingbirds and recording their feeding patterns in your yard or community is an activity the whole family can enjoy together.

National Audubon Society:
Hummingbirds at Home

http://hummingbirdsathome.org

-7-

Learning More

If you want to learn more about these two amazing birds, here are some ideas:

Boring, Mel, 1996, *Birds, Nests, and Eggs*, Minnetonka, MN, NorthWard

Collard III, Sneed B., 2002, *Beaks!*, Watertown, MA, Charlesbridge Publishing, Inc.

Lazaroff, David Wentworth, 1995, *The Secret Life of Hummingbirds*, Arizona-Sonora Desert Museum

Pepperberg, Irene M., 2008, *Alex & Me*, New York, NY, Harper-Collins Publishers

Stewart, Melissa, 2014, *Feathers*, Watertown, MA, Charlesbridge Publishing, Inc.

Stokes, Donald & Lillian, 1989, *Stokes Hummingbird Book*, New York, NY, Little Brown and Company

Wright, Maggie, 2013, *African Grey Parrots*, Hauppauge, NY, Barron's Educational Series

MY NOTES

*"No matter what accomplishments
we make, somebody helps us."*
—ALTHEA GIBSON

Special Thanks to:

Lucile Burt, Poet / Teacher
Wellfleet, Massachusetts

Kathy Dale, Director of Science Technology
National Audubon Society
New York, New York

Margie Lawler, Teacher / Librarian
Beverley Cleary Elementary School
Portland, Oregon

Dr. Michael T. Murphy, Professor
Department of Biology
Portland State University
Portland, Oregon

Leslie Rennie-Hill
Wife and Sharer of Many Good Ideas
Portland, Oregon

9 781944 733391